Zamani Goes to Market

ZAMANI
Goes to Market

by MURIEL L. FEELINGS
illustrated by TOM FEELINGS

Africa World Press, Inc.

P.O. Box 1892
Trenton, New Jersey 08607

to Zamani and Tom

Africa World Press, Inc.
P.O. Box 1892
Trenton, N.J. 08607

First Africa World Press, Inc. edition, 1990

Library of Congress Catalog Number: 88-70729

ISBN: 0-86543-094-2 HB
0-86543-095-0 PB

It was cool in the early morning. The sun spread a soft light over the family compound of five huts.

Zamani was wide awake. He had slept little that night; he was too excited. Today for the first time he would go to market with Father and his older brothers!

He was already dressed when he heard Mother call:

"Wake up, my child. We must get busy."

Mother was cooking over the big pots on the fire. Zamani went to her side and knelt politely. "Have your porridge, then we can prepare," she said, and filled his wooden bowl with ugali.

Zuri, his older sister, came up to him. "Good morning, Zamani." She smiled. "You will not stay with us today."

"No, I am going to market," Zamani said proudly.

In no time his bowl was empty. Looking around, he saw that everyone was busy. Zuri was washing bowls and pots. He saw Father in the distance leading a big steer in from the field. Jenga and Kamili, his brothers, were tying bundles of corn and sacks of cassava.

Mother was gathering clay pots in front of her hut. The large brown pots sparkled in the morning sunlight. Zamani helped her to line them up by size as he had done before. He held each pot steady as she tied them together, neck-to-neck, with heavy string made of sisal plant. Then, carefully, they put them into two straw baskets.

"There!" said Mother, satisfied. "We are finished. Thank you for your hands, Zamani."

"Where may I put these, Mother?" he asked.

Mother pointed to the group of trees at the edge of the compound. "If you can do it, they should be carried out there."

To show everyone how strong he could be, Zamani took hold of each basket and slowly dragged them across the compound until he reached the big trees.

Father was nearby loading bundles on the back of the long-horn steer.

Zamani walked over and knelt politely. "Good morning, Father," he greeted shyly.

"Greetings," Father replied. "Are you now too tired to do more?"

"Oh no, Father," Zamani answered, quickly rising to his feet.

"Well, you will have a big job today. Go to the field and bring the brown calf. You will lead it to market."

The brown calf! Zamani dashed off toward the field, grinning with pride. "So," he thought to himself, "I will take goods to market just like Kamili and Jenga!"

As he reached the fenced pen where the four calves grazed, Zamani's steps slowed. He began to feel a big sadness, too. He had seen other calves go to market when he stayed behind. But the brown calf was special to him. He remembered the early, early morning Father had called him from sleep to see this calf when it was just born.

The brown calf turned and wagged its tail as Zamani approached. He led it out of the pen and through the field, guiding it gently with a crooked stick. As he looked back at the others, he told himself that they would take the calf's place. And more would be born.

Father stood waiting, puffing on his old wooden pipe. Jenga and Kamili lifted the baskets of pots onto their shoulders. Everyone was ready to go.

They called good-bye to Mother and Zuri and started down the path through the village to the main road. Father went first, leading the big steer, with Zamani keeping the calf close behind. Then followed Jenga and Kamili.

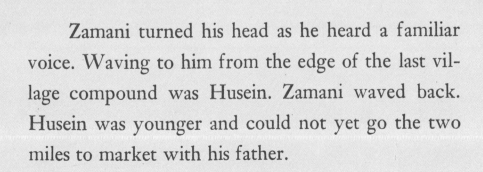

Zamani turned his head as he heard a familiar voice. Waving to him from the edge of the last village compound was Husein. Zamani waved back. Husein was younger and could not yet go the two miles to market with his father.

Along the road were others of their village, also off to buy and sell. Zamani saw men leading cattle, women with babies strapped to their backs and carrying large wide baskets on their heads. One boy of Jenga's age was busy juggling two huge baskets of squawking chickens.

Suddenly Zamani felt a *bump*. It was the calf!
Zamani gave it a pat on the shoulder and kept a
closer watch.

"One half-mile more," Kamili called from
behind.

Nearly there! Holding the calf tight, Zamani darted out into the middle of the road to see what was ahead. He strained his eyes hard, past the crowd, and looked and looked. In the distance, he could see tiny low buildings and other taller ones. "*Kuja, Kuja!*" He urged the calf into a faster pace.

Soon they were walking through the wide street of the town. When they reached the entrance

to the market grounds, the long parade of people went in all directions.

The market was just coming alive. Many vendors were still filling their stalls. Others called: "Good mats!" "Gourds here!" "Good pots!" "Buy here!" Smells of mangoes, pineapples, oranges, and roasting meats filled the air.

Kamili and Jenga went off to sell their pots to those who did not make them.

Father led the way to the far end of the big market where animals were bought and sold. Zamani followed him, guiding the calf through the crowd.

Father stopped at the gate of a tall bamboo fence. Behind it, the sounds of cattle, goats, and chickens could be heard. The brown calf became restless hearing the familiar animal noises. Zamani had to hold it firmly.

A tall fat man came through the gate. He walked around the steer and calf, frowning and touching them here and there, mumbling to himself.

"These are as good as always," Father said.

He offered to sell the corn and cassava also.

The fat man continued to look and touch as
if he hadn't heard. He and Father began to argue
over the price.

Finally, Zamani saw the fat man throw up his hands as if to say, "You win!" Zamani felt proud that his father had won.

The man reached into a large wooden box and

handed Father some paper money. Zamani watched
as he led the steer and calf away. He hoped the calf
would be well cared for and grow up as beautifully
as the steer.

As he and Father walked to the sheltered part of the market, they were joined by Kamili and Jenga.

"Here is the money earned from the pots, Father," said Jenga. The two boys handed him several coins. Father returned three to each, and they ran down the aisle to buy.

"You too have done your share of the day's work," Father said to Zamani. He handed him two coins. "What would you like to buy?"

Zamani looked at the stalls around him. So many things for sale! Straw mats of all sizes and colors. Shoes. Rows of brightly colored ornaments and bead-covered gourds. Stacks of cloth and new kanzus—long, white robes like those his brothers wore. "I don't know yet, Father," he said.

"Well," Father replied, "you will learn to buy wisely today. What do you want most?"

Zamani thought and thought. He stopped before a row of leather sandals of red and brown. He
went to another stall where clean, white kanzus were
hanging. One, his size, was decorated with orange
braid around the collar. Yes, that was just the thing
to buy! It would be his first kanzu.

He turned to tell Father, but then, across the aisle, he saw a beautiful necklace. It was made of three rows of beads—orange, yellow, and white—strung on fine wire into a circular shape. Zamani thought of his mother, who always remembered to bring him sugar cane from the market. He looked back at the kanzu with the orange braid, then at the necklace. Finally he decided.

"I will buy beads for Mother," he said to Father.

"Let us see what the cost is," Father replied. "How much is this one?" he asked the tiny woman behind the counter.

"One shilling, sir."

Zamani looked at the coins in his hand. He had exactly the amount of the necklace. Two fifty-cent coins. "I will buy this necklace," he said to the lady.

She wrapped the necklace in a piece of cloth and tied it neatly with banana-fiber string.

Zamani handed her the coins, then tucked the bundle into the waist of his toga. Suddenly he felt very pleased. He had made his first purchase. He would give his first gift from the market.

Jenga and Kamili joined them, each with a package under his arm.

"You three may head back home," Father said. "I must buy grain for the month and will meet you later on the road."

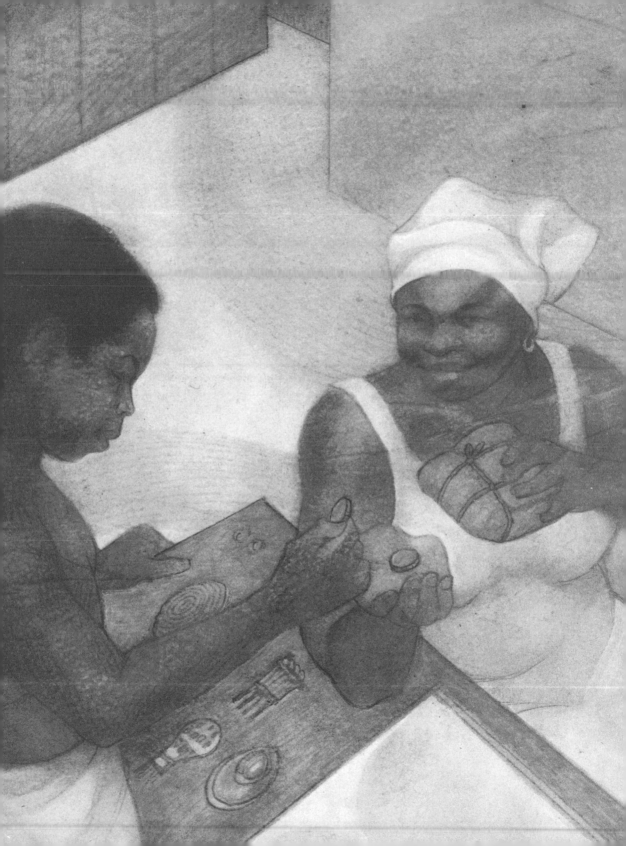

Zamani followed his brothers down the aisle. The market was now very crowded, and they had to weave in and out among the groups of people. Sometimes Zamani bumped against baskets over the arms of busy shoppers. He began to feel very small in that large, noisy market. But, even so, it was fun!

Then they were out of the market and town, and on the road leading home.

It was nearly midday. The soft breezes from the great lake cooled their cheeks as they walked. When the market had grown small in the distance, Zamani remembered the package he had tucked away.

"Kamili, Jenga! See what I bought today!" he cried, boasting. Kneeling down on the ground, he pulled out the flat package from the waist of his toga and untied the string. He carefully unfolded the piece of cloth and held up the sparkling necklace.

"Oh ho! So you wear a necklace now!" joked Kamili, clapping his hands. Jenga laughed too.

"No, no! It is a gift for Mother. Will she like it?" Zamani asked eagerly.

"Oh yes, she will be quite pleased. She has none like it," assured Jenga. "And what else did you buy, little one?"

"That is all," Zamani answered. "What did you bring?"

The boys unfolded their bundles. Kamili had a new straw mat of green and brown. Jenga showed a long white kanzu with orange braid around the neck.

"Just like the one I saw!" Zamani thought, as he ran his hand over the cloth.

Father caught up with them as they were retying their bundles. He was carrying a heavy sack and a smaller bundle.

"You certainly did not get far," he said jokingly. "I thought you would be halfway home!"

As they walked, many people passed them on the left in automobiles, on bicycles, and on foot. Others were also headed back home in their direction. Father greeted villagers and they talked as they went along the sunny road.

At last they were home. Mother and Zuri were preparing the afternoon meal, and the pots were steaming on the fire.

Everyone washed quickly, and Mother served each a large bowl of ugali and stew. She carried one to Father who sometimes ate inside in the heat of the afternoon. Then she returned to the fireside and sat to eat with her four children, and to talk of the news of the market place.

Zamani could not eat his food fast enough. He was anxious to tell his surprise.

"Zamani!" laughed Mother. "Why do you rush so?"

"I must show you something!"

"Well, I hope this *something* will not fly away before you have eaten," she joked, and everyone laughed.

"No, Mother," Zamani answered. He glanced at his two brothers.

Kamili and Jenga smiled at him, put down their empty bowls, and went off to tend the cattle in the field.

Zamani reached into his waistband, pulled out the little flat bundle, and held it out for Mother. "Here is something for you," he said.

"For me?" Mother asked, surprised. She untied the string and unfolded the wrapping. "Oh!" she exclaimed aloud. She held up the bright necklace. "Zuri! Zuri! See what my son has brought me!"

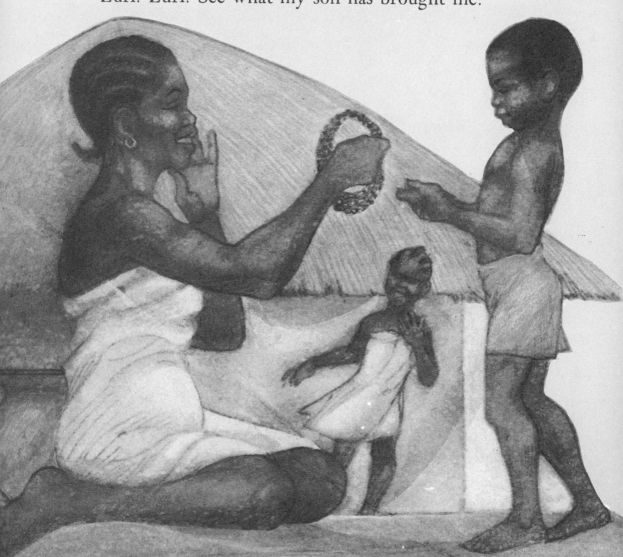

Zuri came and looked at the necklace Mother was proudly holding. "Oh-eh! It was the most beautiful in the market!" she praised.

"Thank you, Zamani," Mother said, and she cupped his face in her hands.

Zamani smiled, with eyes cast downward.

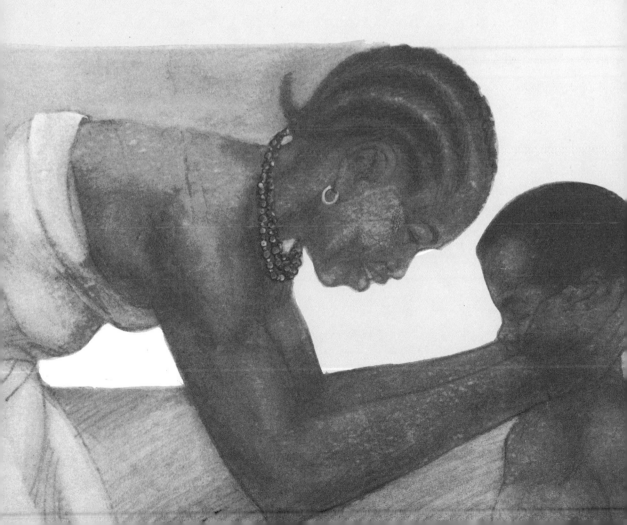

All the family now prepared to go to work. Father, with his hoe over one shoulder, went off to dig in the cornfield. Mother went to her cassava garden nearby, and Zuri was busily scrubbing pots from the afternoon meal.

Zamani's job was to sweep the compound grounds. He went to his hut for the broom.

Inside the cool dark room, he saw a strange object lying on his sleeping mat. His eyes widened as he knelt down to get a closer look. There, on the mat, was a clean new kanzu with orange braid around the neck! Excited, he stood up and held it against his body. It was his size!

He rushed outside, but there was no one to question. He ran back inside and took off his toga. Carefully, he pulled the gown over his head and pushed his arms into the sleeves. He tied it at the neck and walked over into the light of the doorway. Looking down, it was just the right length. He held his head high as he strutted around the hut in his first kanzu. How fine he would look when he entered school.

At last he took off the robe and folded it neatly. As he began to sweep the compound, he thought and thought. How did the kanzu get there? Then he remembered the small bundle Father had carried under his arm. Yes! It was Father! But how did he know?

Zamani covered every inch of ground with his broom, anxious for evening to come when he would thank Father for the surprise gift. He thought of Father in the field, puffing on his old wooden pipe. "A new gift for Father!" he exclaimed, as he swept the last spot of ground.

He sat down in front of his hut. How could he buy Father a pipe? He would have to make things to sell at the market. Yes, that was it. He would ask Jenga to teach him how to make the brown pots.

Zamani picked up his crooked stick and ran off toward the fields to join his brothers and share his plan for the next market day.